Snow Day Surprises

D1403937

This book belongs to

_____

By Jimmy Badavino

Illustrated by Christie Colangione-B

Badavino Creative Studios

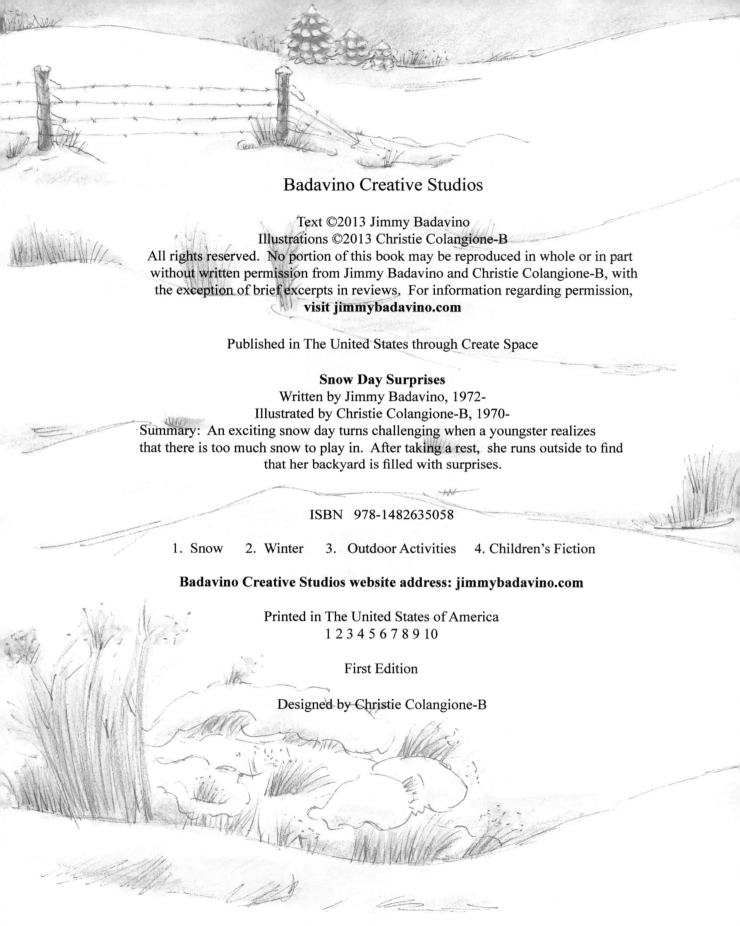

Badavino Creative Studios

Published in The United States through Create Space

Snow Day Surprises
Written by Jimmy Badavino, 1972-
Illustrated by Christie Colangione-B, 1970-

Summary: An exciting snow day turns challenging when a youngster realizes
that there is too much snow to play in. After taking a rest, she runs outside to find
that her backyard is filled with surprises.

ISBN 978-1482635058

1. Snow   2. Winter   3. Outdoor Activities   4. Children's Fiction

Badavino Creative Studios website address: jimmybadavino.com

Printed in The United States of America
1 2 3 4 5 6 7 8 9 10

First Edition

Designed by Christie Colangione-B

To our Children,
Gaetana, Sofia, and Vincenzo

Love, Mom and Dad

Many winters ago, a young girl sat close to the family television set, watching the evening weather report. A huge winter storm was closing in and she hoped to have the next day off from school...

...a snow day she could spend playing outside.

The following morning, school had been canceled, and she thought about the fun activities she would be able to do in all of the newly fallen snow. The youngster was very excited, and quickly changed her clothes and ran down the steps to the kitchen. After eating her oatmeal, she put on her out door clothing...

...and hurried out the door to play in the snow covered back yard.

First, the girl turned and fell backwards into the snow. She tried to make an angel, but the snow was too high, and her arms and legs weren't strong enough to move it around. After a few tries, she became tired...

...so she found something else to do.

Sleigh riding can be a lot of fun. So she
grabbed her toboggan and walked towards a nearby
hill. But the snow was very deep, and her little legs
were getting tired...

...so she found something else to do.

She then decided to build a snowman. First, she packed a small amount of snow between her mittens and patted it into a ball. Then, the girl tried to roll it into a bigger ball, but the snow was quite high and her arms were getting tired...

...so she found something else to do.

Building a fort can be fun, and there sure was plenty of snow for her to make one. It would be big enough for her to sit in, and maybe have her favorite dolly join her for a hot chocolate party. But the snow was very heavy, and shoveling was getting tiring...

...so she found something else to do.

Hot chocolate seemed like a good treat, so she
went inside to warm up and get some rest.
She thought about skating next, but the pond
was too far, and there was a lot of snow to clear.
Playing outside had made her drowsy...

...so she slowly fell asleep.

After a short nap, she decided to go back outside to play. She walked only a few steps, and to her surprise...

...the biggest angel she had ever seen was pressed into the snow.

The young girl then turned around, and to her surprise...

...saw the cutest snow man she had ever seen. He had a warm winter hat and scarf, and his eyes and mouth were made of pebbles.

A little further away, there was a huge pile of snow, and to her surprise...

...there was the biggest snow fort she had ever seen.

Across the yard, next to the old tractor barn,
she noticed that the pond was shoveled off, and to
her surprise...

...there was the shiniest ice she had ever seen.

After skating on the pond...

...and playing in her fort,

...and dancing around her snowman,

...and lying in the snow angel,

she saw her dad watching from the porch.

She smiled at him with an adoring gleam
in her eye...

...and he smiled proudly back.

The young girl ran to her
father and gave him a warm hug.

To her biggest surprise...

...her daddy had a snow day too.

The End

Acknowledgements

To our own childhood memories of the snowy Northeast,
and a special thanks to our children, who have given us so many fun
snow day adventures!
For all of the children who have wished for a snow day home from school.
May they be filled with fun surprises!

Jimmy and Christie

For Bob, the cutest snowman our children have ever made!

The End

Acknowledgements

To our own childhood memories of the snowy Northeast,
and a special thanks to our children, who have given us so many fun
snow day adventures!
For all of the children who have wished for a snow day home from school.
May they be filled with fun surprises!

Jimmy and Christie

For Bob, the cutest snowman our children have ever made!

Jimmy Badavino was born in Troy, N.Y. He attended Green Mountain College in Vermont, and began his literary career with a published novel in 2009. His love for creative writing led to The Santa Clock (2010), That's Why They're Called Punkins (2011), The Ballerina's First Dance (2012), Snow Day Surprises, a screenplay, and further children's stories that are now in production. Jimmy is currently working on his second novel and a chapter book for young readers.

Christie Colangione-B was also born in Troy, and is a graduate of The College of St. Rose in Albany, with a BS in Graphic Design. She is a Designer/Illustrator who has had a life long passion for art. Snow Day Surprises is her fourth children's book. Her first, The Santa Clock, was published in 2010, followed by That's Why They're Called Punkins (2011), and The Ballerina's First Dance (2012). Christie is currently working on several children's stories, and a product line based on the couple's works.

Jimmy and Christie were married in 1996 and established Badavino Creative Studios in 2009. The unique blend of their talents allows them to share their love of family and tradition with others while creating special moments with their three children.

Look for their next children's book due out fall 2013.
To purchase other books, or to find information about upcoming works and other products by Badavino Creative Studios, be sure to visit:

jimmybadavino.com

Badavino Creative Studios

Made in the USA
Charleston, SC
14 October 2015